BASKETBALL BLUES

GO TO
WWW.MYGOGIRLSERIES.COM
FOR **FREE** GO GIRL! DOWNLOADS,
QUIZZES, READING CLUB GUIDES,
AND LOTS MORE GO GIRL! FUN.

Get to know the girls of

GO GIRL!

BY
THALIA KALKIPSAKIS

ILLUSTRATED BY
ASH OSWALD

FEIWEL AND FRIENDS
New York

A Feiwel and Friends Book
An Imprint of Macmillan

BASKETBALL BLUES. Text copyright © 2005 by Thalia Kalkipsakis. Illustration
and design copyright © 2005 by Hardie Grant Egmont. All rights reserved.
Printed in the United States of America. For information, address
Feiwel and Friends, 175 Fifth Avenue, New York, N.Y. 10010.

Library of Congress Cataloging-in-Publication Data Available

ISBN-13: 978-0-312-34646-1
ISBN-10: 0-312-34646-8

First published in Australia by E2, an imprint of Hardie Grant Egmont.
Illustration and design by Ash Oswald.

First published in the United States by Feiwel and Friends,
an imprint of Macmillan.

Feiwel and Friends logo designed by Filomena Tuosta

First U.S. Edition: September 2008

10 9 8 7 6 5 4 3 2 1

www.feiwelandfriends.com

CHAPTER ONE

It's no fun being called a boy.

Even though I don't think I look like a boy, it still feels yuck.

But that's just what happened. Someone called me a boy and everyone laughed.

It was awful.

I don't normally fuss much about how I look. I'm not a *girly* girl—I'm a *sporty* girl . . . a basketball girl. I know I have better things to do than worry about how I look, but still . . .

Here's how it happened.

My basketball team was playing the first game of the season. We're called the Cockatoos and we're a great team. This year, our coach says we might reach the finals.

I love the Cockatoos. My best friend Claire plays on the team, too—we're the only girls on the team. At school, people call us the Basketball Girls because we're both so tall.

The game started out great.

The Cockatoos were winning and we were all playing well. It almost felt like we could read each other's minds.

Then, just after halftime, a boy from the other team tripped, and dropped the ball.

The boy was really short and had bright orange hair. He played with a frown on his face like he would do anything to win, even cheat. But he wasn't a very good player.

I snatched the ball when he dropped it and shot a basket.

Thunk.

"Go, Angie!" Claire yelled.

We slapped our hands in a high five.

I loved scoring for the Cockatoos. We were all running to the other end of the court, when the boy who had just dropped the ball asked me a question.

"Excuse me," he said. "Are you a boy or a girl?"

How rude! He was just saying that because I scored after his turnover. It's not *my* fault he dropped the ball.

So I just looked at the orange-haired boy as if to say, *you idiot*.

But he kept going. "Are you a boy?" he asked. "You play like a boy."

"Yeah?" I said. "You play like a girl!"

Then I ran off.

When you're a sporty girl like me, you have to stand up to idiot boys.

After that, I thought the orange-haired boy would leave me alone. But he didn't. Next, he moved near Claire.

"Excuse me, is your friend a boy or a girl?" he asked Claire.

That's when things started turning bad. I had thought Claire would roll her eyes or stick her tongue out at him. We always say there's no point trying to talk sense to boys.

But Claire didn't do either of those things. Instead, she gave me a funny look, as if the boy was saying something that made sense.

Suddenly, I felt a little worried. I couldn't understand why Claire would look at me like that. The more I thought about it, the worse I felt. I started thinking that Claire's look could mean only one thing.

She thought I was ugly.

CHAPTER *TWO*

I don't remember much of the game after that. At one point the ball whizzed past my face, but I wasn't even looking at it. I don't think I touched the ball for the rest of the game.

All I can remember is a tight feeling in my throat and a whirl of questions.

Did Claire really think I was ugly? Did she think I looked like a boy?

But it got even worse.

At the end of the game, we all started walking off the court. I was feeling really bad and wanted to talk to Claire. She was at the other end of the court with the rest of the Cockatoos.

I started walking towards them, feeling a little left out.

Suddenly, the group stopped walking. They turned to look at the orange-haired boy. Then they looked at me, and laughed.

The whole team was laughing at me. Everyone thought I looked like a boy!

My eyes started burning and I ran to the bathroom, holding my breath to keep the tears inside.

When I was safely in the bathroom, I cried and cried, gulping for air between sobs.

I knew it was silly to worry about how I looked, but I couldn't help it.

When I stopped crying, I pushed some hair over my hot, wet face and sneaked outside. I ran all the way home.

Normally, I walk home with a boy from our team. His name is Tyler and he lives on my street. But I didn't want anyone looking at me now.

All afternoon I moped around in my room. I felt like I had just found out a terrible secret that everyone else already knew. But now I knew it, too.

No one thought I was pretty.

For a while, I stared at my face in the mirror. It was blotchy and red. It didn't look pretty at all.

Then I lay on my bed, staring at the ceiling. I lifted my legs in the air so I could see them above me. They looked long and strong. They didn't look like girly legs. I let them drop on to my bed.

I sighed. I always used to like my legs. Strong, long legs are good for basketball. But I didn't like my legs anymore.

After a while, I rolled onto my side so I could see the photo on my bedside table.

The photo was taken when I was four. In it, Dad is holding me up so I can reach the basketball net in our backyard. I'm holding a basketball, ready to do a slam dunk. Even at that age I had strong arms. I have a really goofy grin on my face.

It's my favorite photo.

Ever since I could walk, Dad has been teaching me to play basketball. He loves basketball even more than I do. He even works for the Tigers.

Dad says he has the best job in the world. I used to dream of working with Dad when I grew up.

But now everything seemed back to front and upside down. Basketball didn't seem so fantastic anymore.

I shut my eyes and rolled away. I wished I could stop being me. I didn't want long legs. I didn't want strong arms.

If being good at basketball made me more like a boy, then I didn't want to play anymore.

CHAPTER THREE

That night I went with Mom and Dad to watch the Tigers play. That cheered me up a little—I love watching the Tigers.

When the Tigers scored, Mom and Dad went wild. Mom waved her flag and Dad cheered like crazy. Even I clapped. When the Tigers are doing well, it's like nothing else matters.

Then a time-out was called.

Music tinkled through the speakers and five cheerleaders ran onto the court. They wore sparkling costumes and punched their pom-poms in the air with power.

I always loved watching the cheerleaders but tonight they looked better than ever. They shimmered across the court as if they belonged in a fairytale world.

They looked exactly how I wanted to look—happy, confident, beautiful.

They looked amazing.

Then I noticed a new dancer. She had long blonde hair, long legs, and a shining smile. She was even more stunning than the others. She was the most beautiful person I had ever seen.

When the time-out was over, I flipped through the program until I found the new dancer. Her name was Sara Shine.

I kept staring at her photo, wondering what it would be like to be her. No one would laugh at her because of how she looked.

At halftime the cheerleaders ran out onto the court again. They wore short white skirts over their glittering leotards, and danced to pop music.

I picked out Sara Shine from the squad. As she twirled, her skirt flowed in a circle around her. She looked like a fairytale princess, cheering for her Prince Charming.

I smiled to myself. Imagine if one of

our players fell in love with Sara Shine! A star basketball player getting married to the prettiest cheerleader—it would be like a fairytale come true. It was such a beautiful dream, I felt dizzy.

As the song came to an end, I leaned closer to Mom.

"Mom, I want to learn to dance like that," I said.

"Like that?" Mom asked, playing with her flag. "No, you don't, sweetheart."

"Yes, I do," I said a bit louder.

Hey, I want to be a cheerleader!

Then Dad leaned past Mom.

"You're not like those girls, Angie," Dad said.

When Dad said that, the tight feeling came back to my throat. But I was too angry to cry.

"Yes, I am!" I whispered.

Inside I was thinking, *I want to be like them. I want to be pretty.*

I took a shaky breath and said, "I want to quit basketball and learn to dance."

Mom and Dad both shook their heads and laughed.

"Quit basketball?" Dad asked, as though I was joking.

Then the game started again, and my parents turned to watch it as if there was nothing else to say.

They didn't realize that I was serious

about this. But I had made up my mind—I was going to quit basketball.

For dancing.

CHAPTER FOUR

The next morning, I lay in bed thinking about the new cheerleader, Sara Shine.

What was it that made her pretty?

She had a nice face, but I couldn't change my face. She also had long hair and sparkly clothes.

I climbed out of bed and started searching through my wardrobe. Under a pile of sweatshirts, I found a skirt that my aunty had given me that I'd never worn before. It was blue with silver swirls on it. I pulled it on.

I felt a little better.

But there were lots of things I wanted to do—grow my hair and buy some new clothes, for starters.

Should I tell Dad how I feel?

And I wanted to talk to Dad about quitting basketball.

I found Dad in the kitchen, drinking coffee and reading the newspaper. I knew he had the sports section because he was so busy reading that he didn't hear me come in.

"Dad, I want to quit basketball," I said.

"Angie!" Dad said, jumping with fright.

Then he laughed at himself for being so surprised.

"Sorry, Dad!" I said, laughing.

"Come and sit down, Angie." Dad pulled out a chair. "What happened at yesterday's game?" he asked, patting the chair.

"Yesterday's game?" I asked.

I wasn't expecting him to ask about that. I stood still.

"Something must have happened," Dad said, "because yesterday morning you still loved basketball."

I looked down at my hands. I didn't know what to say.

Dad stood up and put his hand on my shoulder.

"You can tell me," Dad said. "You'll probably feel better if you talk about it."

"They think I look like a boy," I said, still not looking up.

"Oh," Dad said. "How silly! Kids can be so mean."

I didn't say anything.

"You know what I think?" Dad said. "It's because you're good."

I nodded. I knew I was good. But that was part of my problem—being good at basketball made me seem less like a girl.

It isn't fun for me!

"They're just trying to put you off your game," Dad said. "It's all part of the fun of the game."

It isn't fun for me, I thought.

"When you play serious sports, you have to put up with a little teasing," Dad said. "All the professionals have to get used to it."

I still didn't say anything but I didn't *want* to get used to it. I wanted to quit.

Dad sat down again and patted a chair for me.

"I want to do something that girls do, Dad," I said, as I sat down.

"But you've worked so hard with basketball!" he said. "Why don't you think about this some more?"

I didn't like making Dad sad.

We loved playing basketball together in the backyard—it had always been our special time together.

But feeling like a girl was even more important than playing basketball with Dad. I never wanted people saying I looked like a boy again.

Dad looked at me carefully. "You liked the cheerleaders last night, didn't you?"

I nodded and smiled.

"Let's make a deal," Dad said slowly. "I'll find out about cheerleading at work."

"Yay!" I gave Dad a hug, waiting for the other part of the deal.

"But you can't forget about your team," he continued. "If you want to quit, then you'll have to tell them yourself."

I gulped. I hadn't thought about that. I wanted to hide from my team, to never see them again. I didn't want to have to tell them I was quitting.

How was I going to face the Cockatoos?

CHAPTER FIVE

For the rest of the weekend, I felt scared about telling the Cockatoos that I was going to quit.

I kept thinking about talking to the coach and the team, playing the scene over and over in my mind. But no matter how much I thought about it, I couldn't think of the right thing to say.

I was scared they would laugh at me

and scared of what they would say. I knew that quitting would leave the Cockatoos with only five players. There would be no spare player, so no one would have any time to rest.

By Monday morning, I was even scared of telling Claire about what was going on.

When I got to school, Claire was playing four square with some boys. We usually play four square or soccer or basketball. It's a lot of fun.

"Aaaaangie!" Claire called out, as though she had been waiting hours for me to get to school.

I shifted the weight of my bag on my back, but I didn't put it down. What should I say to Claire?

I usually tell Claire everything. We used to be the same: being tall and loving basketball. Sometimes we pretended we were twins. But I didn't feel the same as

Claire anymore. Claire was pretty. The team hadn't laughed at her.

"Yay!" Claire called out.

She had managed to get one of the boys out. That meant I could play.

But I stood still.

"Come on, Angie," Claire called.

I shook my head. "You can go," I said to the boy who had just got out. "I don't want to play."

The boy moved into his spot, but now Claire was frowning. "Angie!" She looked worried.

I shuffled my feet on the ground, feeling silly. But I didn't want to play sports with the boys today.

I don't want to play with any boys today!

The boys started playing again and Claire grabbed her bag.

"Let's have a talk," Claire said.

She put her arm around my shoulder.

"Sorry, boys," Claire said in a silly voice.

As we walked away, I smiled at Claire. She's such a good friend. After we had walked for a bit, Claire said, "It's that boy from the game, isn't it?"

I nodded. I felt dumb to be so worried

about what that boy had said. But it wasn't just him.

"That boy was an idiot!" Claire said.

"But it's more than that," I said carefully.

I remembered how Claire had looked at me. I remembered everyone laughing. But I couldn't tell Claire I had seen all that.

"You see . . . I want to learn to dance," I said after a while.

"Dancing? Cool!"

Claire did a jiggle around me and kicked her long legs up and down.

I laughed. "And I'm going to quit basketball," I said.

Claire stopped dancing.

"What? You love basketball," Claire said.

She sounded like she thought I had gone crazy. I shrugged.

"I'm going to quit," I said again.

"Angie, you can't!" Claire said. "We're the only girls on the team!"

I sighed. "I don't want to play anymore," I said.

But what I was thinking was, *I don't want to be called a boy*.

We kept talking. But I couldn't find the right words to explain it to Claire.

By the time the bell rang, Claire was kneeling on the ground and clutching my hands, pretending to be an actress in an old movie.

"Don't leave me, Angie!" Claire said in

a funny voice. "Don't leave me alone with those boys!"

I laughed, but I shook my head.

I wasn't going to change my mind.

CHAPTER SIX

On Tuesday night, Mom and I stood outside the basketball gym.

"Are you sure you want to do this?" Mom asked.

I nodded, feeling sick. I just wanted to get this over and done with.

Slowly, we walked inside.

For a moment, I just stood there. I smelled the sharp, rubbery smell of the ball. I heard the squeak of basketball sneakers dodging and darting on the court. The thud of the ball bouncing on the floor seemed to vibrate right through me.

Was I really going to quit?

But then I saw Claire, running down the court and dodging around Tyler, the boy who lives on my street. Everyone was laughing, just as they had at the horrible game. I never wanted to feel like that again. I had to quit.

When the coach saw my mom, he came over to us.

Mom looked at me. "Angie wants to tell you something," she said to the coach.

I gulped. Then I started talking.

I can't remember exactly what I said. I told the coach that basketball had been fun, but I wanted to try something different. It didn't feel the same anymore, and I had decided to quit.

As I talked, I could see the surprise on the coach's face. He even looked disappointed. But I didn't look at him too much. I didn't want to think about everything the coach had taught me, everything I was leaving behind.

At one point I glanced over at Tyler. He was standing on the free throw line, talking to Claire and watching me. He looked surprised. Claire must have told him I was quitting.

I have to quit:

During dinner that night, Dad asked if I had quit.

I nodded. I wondered what the coach had told our team. What did everyone think of me now?

"I had a chat with the dance teacher at work today," Dad said.

I kept pushing my lasagna around my plate. I wasn't really listening.

But when Dad said, "Earth to Cheerleader Angie!" I looked up and put my fork down.

The cheerleaders! Dad must have talked to the cheerleaders at work. My heart was pumping fast.

"You have to be sixteen before you can join the squad," Dad said.

"But can I still learn to dance?" I asked.

"Well, we have a plan, Angie," Dad said.

He looked at Mom. I nodded slowly. This didn't sound too bad.

And it wasn't. The cheerleaders rehearse before every Tigers home game. Dad had arranged to let me watch them rehearse, so I could decide if I really wanted to be a dancer.

I can't wait to watch the cheerleaders rehearse?

"Yay!" I called, punching my fist in the air like a cheerleader.

"But you have to promise to keep your eyes and ears open," Mom said.

"Ask yourself if dancing will make you happy, Angie," Dad said.

If I watched them rehearse for a season, and still wanted to learn to dance after that, then Mom and Dad would let me.

By the end of dinner, I was humming a

song and bopping in my seat. This was fantastic. I even stood up and started kicking my legs and twirling around the kitchen table like a dancer.

I stopped feeling bad about quitting the Cockatoos. I even stopped feeling bad about how I looked.

I was going to meet Sara Shine!

CHAPTER *seven*

On Saturday, Dad drove me to the Tigers game early. I was so excited my cheeks were sore from grinning.

All the dancers were sitting on the court. They were stretching their long legs and arching gracefully this way and that.

I had imagined that the girls would be joking and laughing with the Tigers' players. But I couldn't see any players.

The dance teacher walked over to us, smiling.

"Thanks for this," Dad said to her.

Then he looked at me. "Stay with the cheerleaders and I'll find you before the game, OK?"

"OK," I said.

Then I pointed at my eyes and my ears, to show that I would keep my side of the deal.

It was great watching the dancers rehearse. They had to worry about pointing their toes and kicking their legs. They had to be fit, too, dancing in short, hard bursts. But they also had to smile as though it was easy. It was harder than it looked.

As I watched them, I imagined myself out there, practicing before a big game. I would be a good dancer, moving my body with grace, and twirling like a princess.

It would be like a dream come true!

When it was nearly time for the game, I followed the cheerleaders into the dressing room. At first, I just stood there, feeling like I was in their way.

Then Sara Shine walked up to me.

"I hear you want to be a cheerleader?" she asked kindly.

I nodded, too excited to talk. I was face to face with Sara Shine!

"The pay's pretty bad, but the rest is fun," Sara said, smiling.

I smiled back at her. This was fantastic!

As Sara changed into her costume, she chatted with me about dancing.

"It's good you're starting young," she said, pulling on silky dancing tights. "It takes years of work."

I felt more comfortable after she said that, because it's the same with basketball. You have to practice really hard if you want to be good.

When I started talking about basketball, Sara Shine gave me a funny look.

Suddenly, Sara pulled something out of her bag. "Here, try this on," she said.

I gasped. It was the skirt that Sara had worn as she danced to the pop song.

In a daze, I pulled on the skirt.

Sara rolled it up at the waist so it was the right length.

"Stand back, girls," Sara said to the others. "Angie's going to do a twirl."

With the five cheerleaders smiling at me, I moved to the center of the room and twirled around.

The skirt flowed out in a glowing circle around me, just like it had for Sara Shine.

I kept twirling, dizzy from the glamor and the room rushing past. I felt pretty and girly and very, very happy.

When I stopped, the dancers all clapped. I wobbled a bit on my feet, but I couldn't stop smiling.

As I was taking off the skirt, one of the other dancers called out to Sara.

"How's your dad, Sara?"

Sara glanced at her friend, then looked down at her makeup bag. "He's back in the hospital," she said quietly.

"Oh, Sara."

The friend put her hand on Sara's shoulder. Then they both looked at me.

"I'll tell you about it later," Sara said to her friend.

"It's OK," I said quickly, handing back the skirt. I didn't want to be in the way.

"Thanks for letting me try on your skirt."

Sara smiled. But even behind her stunning smile, I could see how worried she was about her dad. She looked so scared. I imagined how scared I would feel if *my* dad were sick in the hospital.

I started looking forward to seeing Dad before the game. I was glad that he was going to come and find me soon.

And suddenly, I stopped wishing I could be someone else. My life wasn't really so bad. Being pretty wasn't everything.

It doesn't always make you happy.

I suppose I knew that all along.

CHAPTER EIGHT

When Dad came to get me before the game, I gave him a big, squishy hug.

"Hey, Angie!" Dad said, looking pleased and surprised. "How was it?"

"Good," I said.

I wanted to tell Dad lots of things, but mainly that I loved him. "Thanks for letting me watch the cheerleaders," I said.

Dad smiled.

Then he leaned down and kissed me on the head.

"Anything for my beautiful girl," he said.

I smiled back. Then we found our seats and I sat next to Dad, feeling glad we were sitting together. When the game started, Dad and I yelled and cheered louder than ever.

Dad watched the cheerleaders with me when they came on. I told him some of the things I had learned, but I didn't tell him about Sara Shine and her sick dad.

When the game was nearly over, I said to Dad, "Do you know what I like about basketball?"

"I thought you didn't like basketball anymore," Dad said, smiling.

"Well, I still like watching it," I said. "I like watching it *with you*."

Dad nodded. "I hope that cheerleading makes you just as happy," he said.

From then on, I watched the cheerleaders as much as I could. I kept my eyes and ears open like I promised Mom. And, as the weeks went by, I learned a lot.

I learned how fit you have to be to dance, and how to put on makeup. I learned that black clothes make you look thinner and that glittery costumes are scratchy. And I learned that even when she was worried about her dad, Sara Shine still danced as if she was happy.

I think dancing made her happy. In fact, all of the cheerleaders loved to dance.

Will dancing make me happy?

I could see it in their bodies as they sprang across the court or curved smoothly to the music. Moving like that came naturally to them.

Even when they were just talking, the

cheerleaders still moved their legs around or curved their bodies gracefully. It was as if their bodies were always dancing to music no one else could hear.

I started dancing, too. Sara Shine gave me some old dancing clothes, and I would stretch on the floor with the cheerleaders or try to copy their moves as they danced. When she had time, the dance teacher would give me some tips.

It was pretty funny, really, and I tried hard. But I wasn't very good!

The dancers would stretch easily to one side. When I reached across to copy them I'd find I could hardly bend. My body simply didn't move like that.

The cheerleaders made me feel like a girl. They fussed over me and did my hair. They even started calling me their "Little Mascot," even though I'm not little.

It was all working out. I felt like a girl, I did girly things. I even moved like a girl. It was exactly as I had hoped.

And yet, something was missing.

I already knew that life as a dancer

wasn't perfect. Sara Shine's life wasn't a fairytale. But still, something didn't feel right.

Slowly, as the weeks went by, I started to realize something Mom and Dad had known all along—I *liked* dancing. But I didn't *love* it. I didn't want to be a dancer after all.

But what was I going to do now?

CHAPTER nine

One day, toward the end of the season, I was stretching with the cheerleaders. No one knew that I didn't want to be a dancer. I wasn't sure what to say.

But it was still fun stretching. Actually, the dancers were stretching. I was groaning and laughing at how bad I was.

Then two Tigers players came through a side door.

Real-life Tigers players!

I gasped. I was looking at two, real-life Tigers players!

They were talking and bouncing a ball as they walked. They looked relaxed, as if they always had a basketball in their hands.

I glanced at the cheerleaders, but they didn't seem excited to see the players.

I stood up. My heart was beating fast. I wanted to go over to them, and maybe say hello. But I felt shy.

Then I saw Dad walking toward me.

He put his hand on my shoulder. "Do you want to meet them?" he asked.

"You bet!" I said.

Together, we walked over to the players.

"Boys, I'd like you to meet my daughter, Angie," Dad said.

The players stopped and looked up.

"Hey, Angie," one of the players said. "Do you play basketball?"

I gulped, unsure of what to say. But before I could even say anything, he threw the ball to me. It was a hard throw, but I caught the ball easily and bounced it in front of me.

I felt amazing.

Bouncing the ball on a real court brought it all back to me. I realized how much I missed playing basketball.

"I love playing basketball," I said to the player.

I didn't want to let the ball go, but I threw it back.

"Good, solid throw!" the player said.

We chatted for a while and when the players were about to go, Dad asked if we could use their ball.

"Sure," the player said. "You know where to find us."

After that, Dad and I played one-on-one.

We didn't talk much, but we played really well. In some ways, it felt like we were talking by playing together.

I thought about everything I missed about basketball. I missed the rush of air as I raced down the court, bouncing the ball like it was part of my body. I missed that happy feeling when we scored and then clapped our hands in a high five. I missed playing for the Cockatoos.

Dad and I kept playing until the cheerleaders went to get ready for the game.

"Do you want to go with them?" Dad asked.

He tucked the ball under his arm.

I shook my head.

"I realized something, Dad," I said. "I'm not like the cheerleaders. I think I made a mistake," I smiled. "I think I'm a *basketball* girl."

Dad smiled. His eyes were shining.

"Yes, Angie! You are," he said.

It felt good to finally talk to Dad about

I'm a basketball girl again!

this. But I still felt worried about everything that had happened with the Cockatoos. I still didn't want them to say I looked like a boy.

"But I quit, Dad," I said. "I can't go back now."

"Of course you can," Dad said.

He bounced the ball and winked at me.

But I didn't feel so sure. My team had laughed at me. That was the thing that hurt most. We were supposed to be on the same side.

Dad looked at my worried face.

"It's OK," Dad said softly. "It'll work out, Angie."

Then he threw the ball in a huge arc right to the other end of the court. I raced after it.

We played like that, Dad and me, until people started coming in for the game.

CHAPTER TEN

The next morning, I was in the backyard shooting baskets.

Mom called out from the back door. "Tyler's here to see you."

I dropped the ball, surprised. Tyler and I used to walk home from basketball games together, but we didn't really hang out together.

What was he doing here?

Inside, Tyler was holding a basketball. He looked kind of awkward. He had messy hair and a determined look in his eye.

"Want to shoot some baskets?" he asked.

"Umm . . . OK," I said.

We walked outside.

Then, without warning, Tyler threw the ball to me, really hard. I caught it easily—strong arms, solid catch.

Tyler pointed at the ball.

"See how you caught that?" he said. "You were the best player on our team."

I stared at Tyler, shocked. Did Tyler really think I was best on the team?

"But you quit, Angie," he said. He put out his arms like he was asking a question.

"You played one game in the season, then you quit!"

I bounced the ball in front of me, not knowing what to say.

He thinks I'm that good?

"That boy . . . from the first game," I said, as I threw the ball back to Tyler. "He said I play like a boy."

"You *do* play like a boy," Tyler said, laughing. "What's wrong with that?"

But now I was angry. Remembering that first game still made me feel bad.

"You don't know what it was like," I yelled. "Everyone laughed at me!"

You don't understand!

Then, like an idiot, I started crying. I couldn't help it—I still felt awful thinking about that day.

Tyler looked stunned. For a moment, he just stood there.

"Girls are crazy!" he said. Then he muttered, "Umm . . . I've got to go."

He ran down the side of our house and out on to the street.

I started crying even more then. Why was I such an idiot? I felt even worse than at the game. I wanted to run away and hide all over again.

But this time, I stopped myself.

I need my best friend!

I phoned Claire instead.

I don't think I made much sense on the phone. I was sobbing and trying to tell her everything—about how bad it felt to be called a boy and how much I missed playing basketball.

But I must have made some sense, because in a few minutes Claire's mom had dropped her at my house and Claire was hugging me and telling me not to cry.

We talked for real then, like only girls know how to talk, about how we feel deep inside and what we dream of.

And even though I couldn't find the right words to explain it all, Claire seemed to understand.

"That boy only said those things because you're better than him," Claire said.

I nodded. "But it's hard being a girl," I said, "when half the world says you should be pretty and the other half says not to worry."

Claire nodded. Then she said, "But you're beautiful, Angie. I'd love to have your eyes."

And as we talked and joked and laughed, I realized that Claire didn't think I was ugly.

At that game, she'd looked at me the way she did because she understood how I was feeling. It's hard for Claire, too. It's not easy to stand up and be yourself when all the girls on TV are pretty and happy . . . and not at all like real life.

And finally, after all this time, I found out why everyone had laughed as they walked off the court. Claire had said that the orange-haired boy was hopeless at basketball.

Then Tyler had said, "Yeah, he can't play *and* he looks like a Halloween pumpkin!"

So you see, they weren't laughing at me. The Cockatoos were on my side after all.

CHAPTER ELEVEN

After that, I felt *extra* silly for quitting the Cockatoos. But at the same time I felt better about it all, too. I started to realize that Claire wasn't my only friend on the team.

I decided to go and watch the Cockatoos play their last game of the season. They hadn't made it to the finals.

By chance they were playing the team with the orange-haired boy.

It's strange how things work out.

I was excited about seeing the Cockatoos again, but I was also nervous because of the orange-haired boy.

But as I watched him fumble with the ball, I actually started to feel sorry for him. He had such trouble with the ball, I thought how lucky I was to be tall and have strong arms.

I even started feeling bad for saying that the orange-haired boy played like a girl. That wasn't a nice thing to say.

When Tyler saw me up in the stands, he smiled and waved. He seemed glad to see me.

But during the game, Tyler played

differently from how I remembered. He had always been determined, but now he also seemed rough and angry.

If that was how boys played, then I didn't play like a boy at all!

Just before halftime, the orange-haired boy was about to shoot the ball when Tyler suddenly ran right into him. They both skidded on the floor.

It was a really stupid thing to do because now the orange-haired boy would be able to shoot from the free throw line—a free chance to score.

I shook my head. Why would Tyler do something like that?

Then Tyler looked up at me, and I understood why Tyler was playing rough basketball. It was because of me!

Tyler was trying to make the orange-haired boy pay for calling me a boy.

It was Tyler's way of showing me he was my friend.

After months of wishing and dreaming, I finally knew what it felt like to be a fairytale princess.

Sitting up in the stands, watching the game, was like being locked in a tower with Tyler as my Prince Charming.

I felt good that Tyler was trying to be nice, but he didn't have to do that for me. This was *my* battle—I had to face the orange-haired boy myself.

At halftime I went down to the side-lines and found the orange-haired boy.

When he saw me walking up, he looked scared. I could tell he remembered who I was.

But he didn't need to worry.

"You're trying to play like you're tall," I said. "That's why you keep tripping."

The boy looked at me, surprised.

I kept talking. "But you're short and fast," I said. "You should use your speed."

The orange-haired boy opened his mouth to say something, but I just smiled and walked away.

I didn't need to hear what that boy had to say.

Then I went over to the Cockatoos. They were huddled around the coach. For a second I hovered outside the group, feeling strange. I wasn't on the team anymore.

Then Tyler popped his head up. "There's Angie!" he said.

Suddenly, everyone was talking and crowding around me.

"Hey, Angie!"

"You came back!"

Claire stood next to me and squeezed my hand.

I looked at the coach. "I'm sorry I quit," I said. "I didn't mean to. . . . "

I felt silly saying that, but I meant it. The whole season had been a big mistake.

"It's good to have you back, Angie," the coach said.

Then the buzzer sounded for the game to start again.

After that, I stood next to the coach, watching the game and talking to him about next season.

We even talked about some ideas I had to help the team—I had seen a lot from watching up in the stands.

I realized I actually knew a lot about basketball. It felt great.

The coach listened to what I said and even wrote a few things down.

As I stood on the sidelines, I couldn't stop grinning.

Even though I had messed up the season, I still felt good.

Finally, everything felt right. I felt happy in myself again.

I was back where I belonged.

GO GIRL!

If you loved reading about Angie, you should meet the other Go GiRL! girls.

THE NEW GIRL

BY ROWAN McAULEY

Zoe

GO GIRL!

CAMP CHAOS

BY MEREDITH BADGER

Sophie

GO GIRL!

BACK TO SCHOOL

BY MEREDITH BADGER

Chloe

Go Girl! #11

camp chaos

BY
MEREDITH BADGER

"OK, everyone," called Mr. Perelli above the noise. "Ten more problems to do in the last ten minutes!"

Sophie groaned.

This was the longest math lesson *ever*. Usually Sophie liked math, but today she couldn't concentrate.

"I wish the bell would ring," she whispered to her friend Alice.

"Me, too!" replied Alice. "I've got to finish packing for tomorrow."

Sophie felt a shiver of excitement. Tomorrow they were going to school camp. They were staying near a lake and would be going canoeing. Best of all, they were camping overnight!

"I wish it was just our class going," said Marie, who sat nearby. "Mrs. Tran's class

I can't wait to go camping!

is really stuck up. They're going to hate camping!"

"They'll probably freak out if they get a tiny bit of mud on them!" said Alice, laughing.

Sophie didn't know what to say. The thing is, she used to be in Mrs. Tran's class. She started school with those kids and she got to know them all really well. Her best friend Megan is in Mrs. Tran's class.

Sophie and Megan had always thought they would go right through school together. But two months ago the teachers decided to move some kids from each class. Sophie didn't know if she was excited or scared when Mrs. Tran told her she was one of them. Probably a little of both. Everyone in Mrs. Tran's class said that Mr. Perelli's class was rough and mean.

"The boys catch bugs," Megan said, wrinkling her nose. "Then they eat them."

"The girls hang from the monkey bars even when they're wearing dresses," said Katie. "They don't care if their undies are showing."

"And Mr. Perelli yells *all* the time," added Claire.

Sophie's heart was beating fast when she walked into Mr. Perelli's class for the first time. Mr. Perelli was standing at the front of the classroom. He was frowning at something on the blackboard, but when he saw Sophie, he turned and smiled. It was a broad, friendly smile and it made his face look totally different.

"Hi, Sophie," he said. "Welcome to our class! There's an extra seat next to Alice. She'll look after you."

Sophie had seen Alice on the playground. She was tall and strong and spent most lunchtimes playing games. She always had scabs on her knees and grass stains on her clothes.

"She's so rough," Megan had said one day, as Alice went rushing past.

Sophie had nodded. Alice did look a little rough. But Sophie thought that she always looked like she was having fun. . . .